The Adventures of Karen and Bunny-Bunny

Maria Williams

NEWMAN SPRINGS PUBLISHING
320 Broad Street
Red Bank, NJ 07701

First originally published by Newman Springs Publishing 2020

ISBN 978-1-64801-478-9 (Paperback)
ISBN 978-1-64801-479-6 (Digital)

Printed in the United States of America

To Carrie S. Williams

Contents

Bunny–Bunny 2

Karen's Big Secret 6

All Bullies Have Their Day 7

Bunny–Bunny Gets Lost 10

It Is a Process 12

Constructive Criticism 17

The Daydreamer 22

New Neighbors 26

Karen Receives a Letter from Cam 33

Bunny-Bunny

Karen was an only child, born to Andrew and Carrie Willie. They lived in Virginia Beach, Virginia.

On several occasions, Karen had asked for different pets, but Karen's mom did not feel she was responsible enough. Karen's tenth birthday was coming up, and she thought this would be the perfect time to ask her mom for a pet. Karen asked for a dog but was told that there was not enough room for a dog. Karen asked for a bird and was told that birds are too messy.

The next day, Uncle Lui, Mom's baby brother, stopped by the house to see what Karen wanted for her tenth birthday. Karen told Uncle Lui she wanted a pet, but Mom was not excited about the idea. Lui went into the kitchen where his sister, Carrie, was cooking.

Lui said, "Carrie, I want to get Karen a bunny for her tenth birthday."

Carrie said, "I don't think Karen is responsible enough to care for a bunny."

Lui said, "Carrie, Karen is a wonderful child. She's great in school and does all her chores around the house. I really think she has proved herself and would definitely take care of the bunny."

"Okay, Lui."

Uncle Lui said, "Karen, come downstairs. I want to talk to you."

Karen said, "Okay."

Uncle Lui said, "I have convinced my sister that you are responsible and capable of taking care of the gift I have for you for your tenth birthday."

"Oh, Uncle Lui, what is it?"

"So you don't want me to surprise you?"

Karen said, "No, I want to know so I can prepare for the gift."

Uncle Lui said, "Well, okay, I suppose you will need to prepare."

"Please tell me, Uncle Lui."

"Okay, it's a real live bunny."

Karen was so happy. She hugged and kissed her uncle and ran in the kitchen and hugged and kissed her mom. Finally, it was Karen's birthday, and she couldn't wait to receive her gifts. Uncle Lui was the first to arrive at the house. He had the cage in his left hand and the beautiful white bunny in his right arm. The bunny had a pink nose and pink inner ears. Out of all the gifts Karen received, her bunny was the most precious gift.

Mom said, "Karen, what will you name him?"

Karen said, "Bunny-Bunny. That's the name I've already chosen."

Uncle Lui said, "Bunny-Bunny—oh yes, I like it."

The next day, Karen woke up eager to take care of her precious gift. Little did Karen know how much work was ahead for her. Every morning, she had to feed and put water in his cage. Every evening, she had to clean his cage. On the weekend, Karen could not sleep in because she had to do her regular chores and take care of Bunny-Bunny. Karen could not give up because she had promised her mother that she was capable of taking care of her pet.

Sometimes when she tried to feed or clean Bunny-Bunny's cage, he would hop out and take off hopping. She would have to chase him all around the yard. Fortunately, with the help of some grapes, Bunny-Bunny would hop back in his cage. After a while, when Bunny-Bunny settled in, Karen adored taking care of her most precious gift.

Karen's Big Secret

It was another morning in the life of Karen and Bunny-Bunny. Karen went outside to feed him and noticed how huge he had gotten. Karen realized that she would have to ask her parents about getting a larger cage. Karen took Bunny-Bunny out and began to play with him. She jumped around the backyard singing and hugging Bunny-Bunny. Karen sat down and began to talk to Bunny-Bunny.

She said, "Bunny-Bunny, if only you were real. Sometimes I get so lonely and just wish you could talk to me. Sometimes I even feel you understand what I'm saying. Oh, how I wish you could talk to me!"

All of a sudden, Bunny-Bunny said, "I can talk, Karen, but only you can hear me, so you must not tell anyone. It will be our very own secret. I made a wish to be able to talk, but I had to promise to only speak to you. No matter how much you want to tell your friends, I can only talk with you."

Karen was so taken aback by her new friend. She was overwhelmed. She hugged and kissed Bunny-Bunny and told him how much she loved him.

All Bullies Have Their Day

Karen seemed sad this morning when she went out to feed Bunny-Bunny and clean his cage. Bunny-Bunny sensed she was sad. Bunny-Bunny said, "Why aren't you talking to me today, Karen?"

Karen said, "I'm just so scared to go to school today."

"Why?" said Bunny-Bunny.

"John Bubba is the meanest kid in school. He bullies anyone who gets in his way."

"The girls too?"

"Yes."

Bunny-Bunny said, "Why does he do such a thing?"

Karen said, "He tells all the kids if they don't give him their lunch money or even their lunch, he will get them."

Bunny-Bunny said, "Karen, you do know that bullying is not tolerated in the school system and he can get in big trouble? Oh my, there has to be a reason for John Bubba's actions."

"Yes, I was thinking the same thing."

"Although I feel these are simply scare tactics, we must be careful. You see, Karen, all bullies aren't just born bullies. There is a reason why they act that way. Something must have happened in his life to make him act this way. I have a plan."

Karen said, "What is it, Bunny-Bunny?"

Bunny-Bunny said, "Leave my cage unlocked today! We must become 'secret agents.' I'll meet you by the big oak tree beside the school, and we will follow John Bubba home and try to figure out why is he a bully!"

Karen said, "But what if he comes after me today? There is only a few of us that has not had our money taken away."

Bunny-Bunny said, "Oh, don't worry, he won't mess with you today. Think positive."

Karen left the cage unlocked. Bunny-Bunny met her at the school, and they followed John Bubba home.

John Bubba lived two streets across from Karen's house. As soon as John walked up the sidewalk, his mother yelled out, "John, did you get the money for the baby's milk?"

John said, "Yes, Mother."

John seemed different; he was very humble. Karen and Bunny-Bunny knew John was really not a bad boy, but his little sister needed milk, and his mother was pressuring him. Karen and Bunny-Bunny walked home, and there was total silence.

Bunny-Bunny said, "Karen, you have to tell your mother."

Karen said, "I'm afraid I will get in trouble for not coming straight home from school."

"You may get in trouble, but it's the right thing to do. Your mother will know what to do."

Karen rushed in the house and told her mother the entire story. Karen's mother was very upset that she didn't come to her first. Karen's mother said, "Karen, you must never follow anyone. Instead, come straight home and tell me any problems that you are having at school."

Karen said, "I'm sorry, Mom, but can we help John Bubba's family?"

Mrs. Willie said, "I'll meet with the outreach committee at church and have them take milk and food to the Bubba family."

The outreach committee from church visited John Bubba's family and took them food and plenty of milk for the baby. By the end of the week, John Bubba was different. He apologized to all the kids he bullied at school.

Karen said, "Bunny–Bunny, I'm so glad you are my best friend, and I'm so happy that John Bubba is in my Sunday school class because they teach us all about being nice and kind to others."

Bunny-Bunny Gets Lost

Karen woke up this morning wondering what adventures were ahead of her today. She ate breakfast and got dressed. She fed Bunny–Bunny, and they headed down the street to the neighborhood park. Karen saw a few of her school friends and began to play with them.

Bunny–Bunny played for a while and decided to hop over and look at the beautiful flowers in the park. There were so many flowers that he hopped around for a while. Finally, he decided to go back, but he was all turned around. Every way he went was more confusing.

Karen was getting a little tired and looked around where she had seen Bunny–Bunny hopping earlier, but he was gone. She panicked. Everyone decided to help her look for Bunny–Bunny. The other kids were beginning to get tired of looking. As time passed, she noticed she was the only one left looking for Bunny–Bunny!

She called out, "Bunny–Bunny, where are you! It's time to go home and get dinner. Mom will be looking for us! Bunny–Bunny, come out, wherever you are now."

Karen was so tired she began to slow down. She decided to sit down on an old tree stump. Sitting there, she began to think back on when Bunny–Bunny first came to her on her birthday. She thought of how much her life seemed complete with Bunny–Bunny in it. She loved how she received so much attention from him when she came out in the morning to feed him. She loved how, at Sunday dinner, when Uncle Lui came over, he would tell Mom maybe he shouldn't have gotten Karen that bunny because she spends more time with the bunny than her uncle. The entire family, as well as Karen's friends, loved Bunny-Bunny.

Karen held her head down and began to cry. She heard someone calling her.

"Oh, Karen, where are you? I'm lost, and I can't find you. Karen? Karen, where are you?" said Bunny-Bunny.

Karen ran toward the low squeaky voice and found her way to Bunny-Bunny. At last she had found him. She hugged and kissed him. Karen said, "Oh, Bunny-Bunny, I thought I had lost you forever! I missed you so much! Let's go home before Mom comes looking for us."

It Is a Process

Mom packed Karen's lunch today for school. Karen always loved the lunches that were prepared for her. She always knew it would be a healthy lunch. Her mom always packed a sandwich (peanut butter and jelly), fruit (apple, banana, raisins), chips, and water. Sometimes she would put money in the bag for chocolate milk. Karen usually sat beside Debbie, her friend.

Debbie and Karen have been classmates since kindergarten. Karen liked Debbie. She was a lot of fun, but some of the other children would make fun of her because of her weight. Karen's mom would say, "Never judge a book by its cover but by the inside." Debbie always had interesting stories to tell me about her cat who was named *Girly-girl*. Girly-girl got into a lot of trouble all the time.

Sometimes when Karen and Debbie were eating lunch, the kids would call Debbie names, and the girls would continue talking about Girly-girl as if they didn't hear a word the other kids were saying.

Debbie always brought her lunch to school, but she had much more food than Karen did. Debbie would have a sandwich with three slices of bread. The sandwich was usually a cold cut like sliced ham or turkey. The first piece of bread had mayonnaise, a slice of ham, a slice of cheese, another slice of bread with mayonnaise, another slice of meat, and the third slice with mayonnaise. She usually had an apple, cookies, and juice. Sometimes she had potato chips too. Karen noticed that after they ate, Debbie would say she was real sleepy. After lunch, they would go to the restroom and go outside for recess. Debbie wouldn't run around as much as the other kids because she would start breathing really hard.

One day Debbie didn't come to school. Karen thought maybe she was sick from a cold or something. Two days passed, and Debbie still hadn't come to school. Karen asked their teacher if she had heard from Debbie, but the teacher said no.

After school, Karen told Bunny-Bunny that she was really worried about her friend Debbie. She had been absent from school for two days.

Bunny-Bunny said, "Don't worry, Karen. Maybe she has a cold or something."

Karen said, "Okay."

Bunny-Bunny noticed Karen was still sad as she walked toward the house. Karen walked into the house and said, "Hi, Mom."

Mom said, "Hello, Karen, what's wrong? You don't sound like your normal chipper self."

Karen said, "I'm a little worried about my friend at school. She hasn't been to school in a few days."

"What do you think is going on with her?"

"Mom, I don't know. She is never absent from school. Remember my friend Debbie? Both of us always get the Perfect Attendance Award every year."

Mom said, "Oh yes, Karen, I remember. She is the one that the kids tease about her weight."

Karen said, "Yes, Mom." Karen begin to cry.

Mom said, "Don't cry, Karen. I'm sure she will be okay."

Karen woke up early today, eager to see if Debbie would return to school.

Mom said, "Karen, how are you feeling this morning?"

Karen said, "Mom, I'm okay. I'm just hoping that my friend Debbie comes back to school today." Karen went out the back door and said, "Good morning, Bunny-Bunny. How are you today?"

Bunny-Bunny said, "No, Karen. Most importantly, how are you today? I know you were very worried about your friend Debbie yesterday."

"Yes, I am worried. I'm hoping she will return to school on today."

Bunny-Bunny hugged Karen. Karen rubbed his head, and off she went to school.

Karen walked in class, and there she was—Debbie was sitting in her desk. Karen smiled and said, "Debbie, I was so worried. Are you okay?"

Debbie said, "Yes, we will talk at lunch. I'm on a diet. My weight is causing me to be sick!"

Karen could hardly wait until lunch to hear what had happened to Debbie. Finally, it was lunchtime. Karen said, "Debbie, what happened?"

Debbie said, "Remember at recess how I was tired and could barely breathe after running around?"

Karen said, "Yes."

"I felt really bad when I went home on Friday. Mom decided to take me to the doctor's office on Saturday. The doctor had a technician come in the room and run some tests on me. Mom said the test showed that the overweight problem I have was causing me bad health problems."

Karen said, "So what does all of this mean, Debbie?"

"I have to go on a diet and exercise more."

"What kind of diet?"

"My doctor wants me to eat lesser and healthier. Our doctor referred Mom to a nutritionist."

Karen said, "What is that?"

"A nutritionist is an expert in helping people like me understand the importance of eating food that is healthy and gives your body what it needs to function properly."

"Wow, that sounds really interesting! How did you learn so much so quickly?"

Debbie said, "Our doctor's office set us up with an appointment to talk with the nutritionist on Tuesday. That's why I was out for two days."

Karen asked, "So what do you have to eat now?"

"For example, today I have a peanut butter and jelly sandwich with two slices of wheat bread. For snacks, I have an apple and water. It doesn't seem like enough, but Mom said I will get used to it. Also, I have to exercise."

"What kind of exercise?"

Debbie said, "Mom and I will work out when I get home from school, and we will walk around the neighborhood. I think it will take forever for me to get healthy and lose weight."

Karen said, "Debbie, don't worry. It will happen."

"How can you be so sure, Karen?"

"Because Grandma Willie and my dad both have cholesterol problems."

Debbie asked, "What's that?"

Karen replied, "That's a problem where they can't eat certain foods and have to watch their weight, or they can end up with serious health problems like heart attacks."

"Karen, you are scaring me!"

Karen explained, "No, listen, I heard Grandma Willie tell Dad when he was worried about losing weight and eating healthier something that I will never forget."

"What was that, Karen?"

Karen expounded, "Grandma said, 'Son, listen to me. It took you forty years to get overweight, which is a lot of time. Losing weight and changing your present eating habits are not going to happen overnight. It took time for this problem to happen and it will take time for it to go away. Son, *it's a process.* It will take time, but I know you can do it.' And guess what—my dad did it! And that's how I know you will do it!"

Debbie said, "Cool beans!"

Karen smiled.

Constructive Criticism

Karen loved school. Her favorite class was English and reading. Karen was an excellent reader. There were a few classmates who found reading very challenging. The problem was, they could read, but sometimes they couldn't comprehend (they couldn't grasp the understanding of what they read). The classmates who found reading very challenging would spend one hour once a week in Mrs. Willoughby's class.

Mrs. Willoughby was a pretty tough teacher. Karen's mom said, "If she were a doctor, one would say she doesn't have a great bedside manner." Karen was allowed to assist Mrs. Willoughby weekly on Wednesdays. Her mom said, "It's easy to remember my schedule." She wrote WWW (Weekly Wednesday Mrs. Willoughby) on her calendar!

Nadine Ashby was one of Karen's classmates whom she loved to help with reading. Mrs. W found Nadine very difficult and sometimes tiresome to deal with. Mrs. W said Nadine was a smart-mouth. Karen asked Mrs. W what she meant by "smart mouth." Mrs. W said, "Nadine says things with no regard of how it affects others." As time went on, Karen realized what Mrs. W meant.

One day in class, Mrs. W was explaining something to Nadine, and Nadine turned her head. Mrs. W asked her, "What's wrong? Why did you turn your head?"

Nadine shook her head and shrugged her shoulders, as if to say, *Nothing's wrong.*

Mrs. W insisted, and Nadine said, "Your breath smells."

Mrs. W walked away very upset. Karen was embarrassed and acted as if she didn't hear Nadine's comment.

After school, Karen told Bunny-Bunny about the incident, and he said, "Karen, children rarely think about how something they say sounds to others. They just speak the truth. Haven't you ever heard that phrase 'out of the mouths of babes'?"

Karen said, "No."

Bunny-Bunny said, "It simply means children don't dress things up or think about how harsh something sounds—they just say it. Some children are taught and disciplined at an early age as to what is appropriate or acceptable to say to others, especially adults. These lessons of what to say are taught at home and school at an early age. These lessons are very important because they teach you to respect others."

"Mrs. W was very, very upset. She stormed away from Nadine's desk."

"What did you do, Karen?"

"I turned my head and acted like I didn't hear or see what had happened!"

Bunny-Bunny said, "Mrs. W could have apologized and went and put a mint in her mouth. There is no easy way to tell someone they smell. The main thing is, when Nadine shook her head and shrugged her shoulders, Mrs. W should have known that it was something difficult for Nadine to say."

Karen said, "Sometimes I think that's why Mrs. W lets me work with Nadine because she never knows what she might say."

"Everyone is special, and we all have our challenges, but we must remember that we are to be compassionate and patient with the less fortunate. Also, teachers are not perfect. They don't always respond appropriately as well, but they are human and have a great responsibility. They are equipped with knowledge and tools to help you learn your lessons."

"You are right, Bunny–Bunny. I love school and my teachers."

Bunny–Bunny said, "Karen, there is another thing I want to mention.

Karen asked, "What's that, Bunny–Bunny?"

"Experience is a great teacher, and teachers have a lot of experience."

Next Wednesday, when Karen went to class, Mrs. W seemed different. She was working with Nadine a little more than usual. Nadine raised her hand, and Karen went over to help her. Mrs. W said, "I'll help her, Karen." Mrs. W bent over to help Nadine, and Karen turned her head because she didn't know what Nadine would say. To Karen's surprise, Nadine and Mrs. W were smiling.

Karen couldn't wait to get home and tell Bunny–Bunny what happened in Mrs. W's class today. Karen said, "Bunny–Bunny, you won't believe what happened in school today."

Bunny–Bunny asked, "What?"

Karen said, "Nadine raised her hand for help, and Mrs. W told me she would help her. I turned my head because I didn't know what Nadine would say, but to my surprise, when I turned around to look, they were both smiling."

Bunny–Bunny said, "I think Mrs. W thought about the situation that happened last Wednesday and knew that she could have handled it better. She probably decided to handle the constructive criticism with a positive response this time by using a breath mint or mouthwash! What a great outcome!"

Karen agreed, "Yes, what a great outcome!"

The Daydreamer

It was Saturday morning, and the sky was gorgeous. The clouds were puffed up like popcorn. Some of the clouds shadowed other clouds, and behind the shadows was a brightness where more clouds sat. Karen was imagining what those clouds looked like over the beach. She went out to see Bunny-Bunny and said, "Hi, Bunny-Bunny, how are you doing today? Isn't the sky just beautiful?"

Bunny-Bunny said, "Yes, it is."

Karen fed Bunny-Bunny and gave him some water and sat down on the grass gazing up at the sky. She lay back as Bunny-Bunny ate. She stared up at the clouds in a daze as she drifted away. She was wearing a silk pink dress with white tights and ballerina shoes. Bunny-Bunny was behind her, floating on the clouds too. Beautiful music was playing. She could hear each instrument in the song. It was music she had never heard before. Bunny-Bunny was dancing with her in the clouds. She was watching her mom and dad talking and laughing. Mom and Dad seemed so peaceful. Dad wasn't dressed up in dirty work clothes. Mom didn't have on her usual clothes either. Dad didn't look like he was worried about getting all the cars repaired that had passed the deadline for being fixed. Mom was not going from room to room cleaning the house. She was not looking at what menu she would be preparing tonight for dinner. She wasn't separating the clothes to wash. And on this special day, she had put on makeup, which was rare.

Her mom said that her Mema said she had natural beauty; she didn't need makeup. If Mom was going to a special event, she would wear makeup. Karen was trying her best to figure out what the special event was. As Karen floated around, she noticed quite a few other things.

Papa and Mema were in the clouds. Grandma Willie was there too. Karen looked around, and there were lots of children she didn't know. To her surprise, there was a lake. The lake was beautiful. It was crystal clear. She said to Bunny-Bunny, "Let's go closer and look in the lake."

As Karen and Bunny-Bunny bent over, they could actually see their faces as if the lake was a mirror. The lake was as clear as glass.

Bunny-Bunny said, "I have never seen anything like this lake. It is so beautiful." Bunny-Bunny touched the glasslike lake and exclaimed, "Wooo, it's hard."

Karen touched it and said, "It feels like a glass floor."

Bunny-Bunny jumped in the lake, and Karen shouted, "No, Bunny-Bunny! You might sink down in the lake!"

Bunny-Bunny said, "Come in, Karen, it's not a watery lake. It's a crystal lake like a hard surface floor. Come in! Come in, Karen."

Karen tiptoed lightly onto the crystal floor. Bunny-Bunny said, "Karen, come dance with me."

She looked up, and all the children she had seen earlier were like little angels dressed in pink with wings. They were all around the edge of the lake completing the entire circle around it. Karen felt safe, so she danced around and around with Bunny-Bunny. Mom and Dad joined them on the lake as they danced around. Papa stepped onto the lake and held both of his hands outward. Mema and Grandma Willie grabbed his hands, made a circle, and danced too. Karen looked over and saw Uncle Lui and Aunt Maria dancing. The big surprise was Aunt Lammie dancing gracefully as a professional ballerina. This was a miracle as Aunt Lammie had died at age ten of a crippling disease called muscular dystrophy. Uncle Lui and Mom never talked about Aunt Lammie. Sometimes Karen would see Mom in her room looking at old pictures of Aunt Lammie and crying. Mom told me that Aunt Lammie's name came from Mema who said she was her little Lamb. To see Aunt Lammie dancing was such a wonderful thing. Everyone was crying, but the angels were smiling. I figured out why Mom was crying.

Karen's mom told her that when Aunt Lammie got really sick, she would have to use a wheelchair to get around. Mom said she used to wish that she and Aunt Lammie could dance again like they did before she couldn't walk anymore. Karen figured her mom finally got her wish. Karen thought the angels were rejoicing.

"Karen! Karen!" Mom shouted.

Karen said, "Yes, Mom, what's...what's..."

Mom said, "Are you okay?"

"Yes, I think so..."

Mom said, "You must have been *daydreaming*! It must have been a great dream because you were singing and smiling."

"Mom, I thought dreams happened at night while you are sleeping."

"No, Karen, daydreams occur while you are awake during the day."

"Mom, this was a heavenly daydream!"

New Neighbors

As the sun shone through her bedroom window, Karen stretched and smelled the aroma of coffee brewing. She opened her bedroom door as she rubbed her eyes. She heard her dad talking about the new neighbors across the street who were unpacking their van. She peeked out the front window and saw a boy playing with a puppy. She went in the bathroom, washed her face, and brushed her teeth. She walked in the kitchen, and as usual, her dad said, "Good morning, sunshine."

Karen said, "Good morning."

Mom said, "We have new neighbors."

Karen replied, "I saw them out the front window'. I saw a boy playing with a puppy."

Mom remarked, "I think they have two children. One looked older than the other."

Karen asked Mom if the older one was a girl or boy. To her surprise, the older child was a girl. Mom said she looked like she could be twelve or thirteen years of age.

Karen couldn't wait to eat breakfast, do her chores, and meet the neighbors. She went outside to feed Bunny-Bunny and clean his cage. While cleaning his cage, she told Bunny-Bunny that there were some new kids on the block, and they had to go welcome them to the neighborhood. Karen let Bunny-Bunny back in the cage and started toward the neighbor's house when Bunny-Bunny said, "Karen, why can't I go with you to meet the neighbors?"

Karen said, "They have a dog, Bunny-Bunny, and I don't want the dog barking at you."

Karen started walking across the street. The boy was tossing a ball to the puppy, and Karen said, "Hello, neighbor. My name is Karen Willie."

The boy answered, "Hello, I'm Jacob Cam, how are you?"

Karen sat down on the grass, and they talked for an hour or more. Then Karen heard her mother calling her to come home for lunch.

Karen went to the backyard to give Bunny-Bunny water and started talking about her new friend *Cam*. Karen said, "He's really a lot of fun, Bunny-Bunny. He's only here for a few days, and he's spending the summer with his aunt in Raleigh, North Carolina. You know, I think he has been all over the world. His dad is a salesman. Cam said his dad promotes this special attachment to the world's greatest name in vacuum cleaners, 'Wamster.' Cam said his dad has to sell a certain number of these attachments and then off they go to another state."

Bunny-Bunny said, "How long does his family stay in a state?"

Karen said, "Cam said six months to a year."

Karen gave Bunny-Bunny food and water and went into the house to get her lunch. It was so hot Karen decided to go to her room and lie down. When Karen woke up, it was after 4:00 p.m. She looked out the window to see if Cam was outside, but she didn't see him or Tuna, his dog. Karen went in the kitchen and asked her mom if she had seen Cam outside. Karen's mom said no. Karen went back outside to check on Bunny–Bunny, and he was hopping around in his cage. There was Cam and Tuna, who was jumping around outside the cage.

Cam said, "Hi, Karen. I decided to walk over and see your favorite friend. You talked so much about Bunny–Bunny I couldn't wait to see him. Bunny–Bunny is a happy pet."

Karen laughed and said, "Yes, he is always happy and hopping around." She was surprised that Bunny–Bunny and Tuna got along so well. Bunny–Bunny was happy that he got to meet the *mutt*, at least that was the type of dog Cam said Tuna was.

Karen, Cam, Tuna, and Bunny–Bunny took a walk through the neighborhood.

Cam said, "Karen, I wish I could stay here this summer, but it's a family tradition for me to go to my aunt's for the summer."

Karen said, "We have so much fun here for the summer. We have CFD."

"What is CFD?"

"CFD is 'community family day.' That's when the entire community comes together and have games, food, and fun. We have bake–off contests. Mr. Meekins has a contest every summer at the pet shop. Last year, Bunny–Bunny won his cage/house. Bunny–Bunny really doesn't like for me to call it a cage."

Cam said, "It really is the largest bunny cage I've ever seen."

Karen explained, "Roadsville is the best town in Virginia. My mom was born and raised in Virginia Beach." She said her mom went to the beach almost every day in the summer. "Mom said my grandma would take a book and let her sisters play in the sand and water all day. Mom said Grandma had a love for the ocean. Grandma would say there is just something tranquil and peaceful when you listen to the waves.

Mom said the waves would gather way up high and come down gushing toward the sand white and sudsy. Grandma said the white sudsy stuff was the saltwater we have on the East Coast. Grandma took my mom, and my mom took me to see the sunrise over the ocean, and it was amazing. When the sun comes up, it covers the entire ocean from as far as you can see from one side to the other. Once the sun moves upward, it appears to get smaller and travel. Grandma said, 'Sunshine, this is free, priceless, and one of *God's* many beautiful creations.' She would say, 'Don't ever take this moment for granted.'"

Cam said, "I hope I get to see it before I leave to go to North Carolina."

On their way back to Karen's house, Cam said, "Karen, isn't that your mom leaving my house?"

Karen said, "Yes, Mom baked a pie, took it over to your house, and welcomed your family to the neighborhood—and I'm sure she didn't miss the opportunity to invite your family to our church. I better go now. It's getting dark."

Cam said, "Okay, I'll see you tomorrow."

Karen went in the house smiling and talking about the great day she had. Karen asked her mom if she would take Cam and her to the beach tomorrow. "Mom, he has never seen the ocean, and he really wants to see it."

Mom said, "Karen, I'll check with his mother tomorrow and see if she will allow me to take Cam to the beach."

Karen's mom was up early putting clothes in the washer. She looked out of the window and saw Cam's mom. She walked over where Cam's mom was sitting on the porch sipping coffee. Mrs. Willie said, "Good morning, Mrs. Cam, how are you this morning?"

Mrs. Cam said, "It's a beautiful cool morning. How are you?"

Mrs. Willie said, "I'm great. I was wondering if Cam could go to the beach with Karen and me today?"

"Of course! I wanted him to enjoy these few days here because he will be traveling to spend the summer with his aunt in Raleigh, North Carolina."

"I will pick up Cam in about an hour."

When Karen's mom went back in the house, Karen was already up and dressed. Karen said, "Mom, where have you been?"

"I walked over and asked Mrs. Cam if Cam could come with us to the beach today."

"Did she say he could, Mom?"

"Yes!" Mrs. Willie prepared the picnic basket and cooler with water ready to go. "Karen, bring your cap and sunglasses."

Karen's mom beeped her horn, and out came Cam with his sunshades on, jumping all the way to the car. The beach was only a few miles away. Mom was trying to find a parking space and Cam saw the ocean and screamed out, "Wow!" There were people everywhere. Cam was so excited, and as soon as Mrs. Willie found a parking space, Cam jumped out the car, raring to go.

Karen, her mom, and Cam grabbed the beach chairs, picnic basket, cooler, beach ball, and umbrella. They found a great spot on the sand and sat everything down.

Karen said, "Cam took off into the water."

Mom had her book, and Karen and Cam had their beach ball. Karen and Cam made sand dunes and buried themselves in the sand. They played tag as they ran back and forth on the beach. Three hours had passed. Karen and Cam ate sandwiches and drank cool water. Mom said it was time to start packing up.

On the way home, Cam said he had never had so much fun. "Thank you, Mrs. Willie. The beach was awesome!"

Mrs. Willie said, "Cam, it was my pleasure for you to join us today, but there is one thing I want you to remember. This is an experience that you should never take for granted. Remember the ocean is priceless and one of *God's* beautiful creations."

Cam looked at Karen and smiled. He remembered that Karen had told him what her grandmother said to her when she took her to the ocean to see the sunrise. When Karen's mother dropped Cam off, he ran toward his mom, smiling all the way to the front door.

Karen said, "Mom, thanks for taking us to the beach today."

Mom said, "Karen, you know the ocean soothes me while I read my book."

"I know, Mom, but we had so much fun! I can't wait to tell Bunny–Bunny."

Karen went to the backyard and told Bunny–Bunny all about her day at the beach. Karen started getting tired and went inside to take a shower and get ready for dinner.

It was the next day, and Cam was leaving to go stay with his aunt. Karen was a little sad. She told her mom she didn't want Cam to leave because they had such a good time in such a little amount of time.

Mom said, "Karen, you have to treasure the time you had with Cam. He will be back from his summer vacation with his aunt before you know it. Now, Karen Willie, you march over there and spend as much time as possible with Cam before he leaves."

Karen thought about what her mom had said and walked over to Cam's house with Bunny-Bunny. Cam and Tuna were in the backyard playing. Karen and Bunny-Bunny joined them by jumping around in the yard. Soon Cam's mom called out and said it was time to get ready to go. Karen stood there not knowing what to say.

Cam said, "Karen, this has been the greatest few days I've had in a long time. Mom bought me some stationery, and I promise to write you. Also, I have your phone number, and I promise to call you."

Karen smiled and said, "See ya soon."

As Karen walked back home, she was very quiet.

Bunny-Bunny said, "Karen, don't be sad. It was a wonderful adventure you shared with Cam at the beach."

Karen said, "That's true. I will treasure those memories forever."

Karen Receives a Letter from Cam

Karen saw the mailman and went to get the mail. The mailman said, "Hi, Missy Willie, how are you today?"

Karen said, "I'm great."

The mailman said, "Looks like there is an envelope for you today, young lady."

Karen looked at the envelope, and it was from her neighbor Cam. She ran in the house. Trying to catch her breath, she shouted, "Mom! Mom, Cam sent me a letter!"

Karen's Mom was so happy Cam wrote the letter because Karen had been a little sad since he left three weeks ago. Karen said, "Mom, I'm going outside to read the letter to Bunny-Bunny."

Her mom sort of looked at her funny. She must have thought that was crazy since Bunny-Bunny can't really understand, but little did Mom know Bunny-Bunny *could* understand every bit of Karen's letter from Cam. The letter read,

Hi, Karen and Bunny-Bunny!

I really miss you guys. Although I'm having fun at my aunt's, I still think about the fun we had at the beach.

I've been finding out about the habitat of birds in North Carolina. It's real exciting! My uncle is the one who has been teaching me about the birds. Did you know that the hummingbirds can travel some ninety miles per hour? I found out that these little birds are pretty speedy. These birds are so small. They can fly backward too. North Carolina is really beautiful, and there are so many things to do. I'm taking lots of pictures to show you when I get back. I really think Tuna is homesick because he has been moping around for weeks. Well, I know we were only in Virginia for a few days, but Tuna's not jumping around like he did when he was around Bunny-Bunny in Virginia.

Karen said, "I told you, Bunny-Bunny! Tuna really loved being around us."

Bunny-Bunny said, "Keep reading, Karen. I am so excited to hear from Cam and Tuna."

"Okay. Where was I?"

My uncle took me camping, and boy, did I have fun. We slept in a tent and built a campfire. My uncle loves to fish. He would fish all day, and he would cook the fish on the campfire at night for dinner. I heard owls at night. Sometimes I heard other noises, but I wasn't sure of what the noises were. My uncle would laugh and tell me the noise I heard was bears. One night while we were sleeping, it rained so hard, and we slept soooo soundly.

The next morning, our food supply was trashed. It was as if someone came and opened all our food packages and left the paper all over the campground. Uncle Rae said, "It was probably a hungry bear, but better our food than us!"

We were supposed to go to the museum, but I begged my uncle to go fishing instead. It was the last day of our camping trip, and Uncle Rae said I popped up out of my sleeping bag like popcorn. It was really early, and we headed out to the pier. My uncle said there was such peace out on the lake. I was bored at first, but after a few days, hours would pass, and the only time we talked was when we were reeling fish in. Sometimes if the fish were biting good, we would stay out on the water all day! Uncle Rae would always say, "It's nothing like fresh caught fish!"

I love camping, but I was glad to get back to my room at Uncle Rae's house. Our first night back, there was a terrible storm. My uncle said that Virginia and North Carolina has bad storms. Uncle Rae said he wanted to be a weatherman so when he was younger, he researched storms. Uncle Rae said that to understand what a storm is, we need to know the true definition. Uncle Rae said, "A storm is an atmospheric disturbance manifested in strong winds, accompanied by rain, snow, hail, and other precipitation and often by thunder." Uncle Rae knew I was scared of storms, but he said, "Always remember, normally lightning will strike and light up the sky with an electrical-like sound, but quickly after that happens, a loud thunder will roar. Brace yourself for that crackling noise."

I mean the lightning was so sharp it lit up the entire house. Tuna was barking and whimpering throughout the entire storm. The rain continued for hours. I fell asleep and didn't wake up until the next day.

I told my Aunt Sharon and Uncle Rae all about you and Bunny-Bunny. He said that he would like to meet both of you when he drops me off in Virginia. Well, I'll write you soon. Tell Bunny-Bunny I said hi.

Karen Visits Her Grandparents

Maria Williams

Contents

The Wise One 42

Hard Work with Great Rewards 48

Sara's Jealousy 50

The Wise One

It was Saturday morning. Karen was all packed. Dad was driving Karen and Bunny-Bunny to North Carolina to see her grandparents. The trip was only an hour drive. Bunny-Bunny hated traveling. He felt sick in the stomach quite often. Mom had been packing for Karen and Bunny-Bunny for weeks. Dad had to sit on the luggage to close it. Dad always said, "Honey, she's only staying for two weeks, not a month." Dad had a special cage for Bunny-Bunny when traveling. "Between your luggage and Bunny-Bunny's cage, it's as if we had three passengers in the back seat." Dad would put in and take out the luggage two to three times. Everything had to fit exactly right.

Mom packed snacks and water. As soon as the family sat in the car, they automatically got hungry. Mom packed peanut butter and jelly sandwiches, apples, carrots, chips, water, and punch. Mom said Dad had their trip to Papa and Mema's down to a science. They stopped halfway at the rest stop. They sang "Row, row, row your boat." Each of them took turns jumping in with row, row, row your boat before they got off-track. Karen always blinked at Bunny-Bunny because they would sing "Row, row, row your boat" when no one was around. Bunny-Bunny loved to sing. Karen always felt guilty that he couldn't sing with all of the family together.

Finally, they were turning into the driveway from the entrance gates. Papa and Mema lived all the way in the back of an old dirt winding road. Papa had a garden area where he once grew potatoes, collards, corn, and tomatoes. He had pear and apple trees. Mom said many years ago, they were fed by Papa's crop. Mom said, "Karen, we had to get up early in the morning to help work in the fields."

Karen said, "Yes, Mom, like me with cleaning and feeding Bunny-Bunny."

Mom replied, "No, Karen, we *worked*. Your Papa didn't believe in lying in bed late. We had to get up very early like 6:00 a.m., before the sun came up."

There was Papa and Mema standing at the front door. They were smiling, and Bunny-Bunny was hopping up and down. Bunny-Bunny wanted out of his cage. Papa and Mema loved Bunny-Bunny, but they had too many critters and stray dogs and cats in the area that they didn't like Bunny to stay outside. Bunny-Bunny stayed on their porch, which was kept locked at all times.

Papa and Mema hugged Karen so tight she closed her eyes. She felt like a sponge absorbing a lot of water, but in this case, the water was *love.*

Papa said, "Hey, little squirt, how you doing? And how about your bunny? I wanted to say 'little bunny,' but he has really grown."

Karen said, "We're great, Papa."

Mema said, "There's my sunshine! Sugar, you would brighten up any dark day."

Karen said, "Hey, Mema!" And then came the smothering hug. It was wonderful.

Papa and Mema's house had this porch that wrapped all around the house. The house was two story, but Papa and Mema rarely went upstairs. They had a very large bedroom on the first floor. There were three large bedrooms and two bathrooms on the second floor. Karen's room was upstairs. She loved it upstairs. When she looked out her bedroom window, she could see all around the neighborhood. Mama, Aunt Lammie, and Uncle Lui lived in this house their entire childhood.

Dad brought up Karen's luggage, and Mom started unpacking her clothes and putting them in the dresser drawers and closet. Dad was downstairs talking to Papa.

Mom said, "Papa loves Dad because he was a businessman. He owned his very own mechanic shop. Papa was in the military for a while. When he got out, he raised crop. Papa admires any man who works and takes care of his family."

Bunny-Bunny was on the porch enjoying hopping from one side to another. Mema was in the kitchen preparing lunch. They always had freshly squeezed lemonade or cold tea. Mema prepared a salad with fresh vegetables from her garden. The cucumbers and tomatoes were so good. They had chicken salad and watermelon for desert. After they ate, Mom did the dishes, and they all sat in the den. Mema asked Dad what he was going to do with Karen and Bunny-Bunny away for two weeks.

Dad said, "I'll get caught up at the shop, and then I'll take the love of my life out on the town. I'm getting a little tired, so we better hit the road."

Even though Karen loved visiting Papa and Mema, she always had to fight back the tears when her mom and dad pulled out of the driveway. She would run down beside the car; then her dad would leave her in a heap of smoke from the dirt road. She would watch the car until she couldn't see it anymore.

Karen and Bunny-Bunny just stayed down by the long winding road. It was total silence. They both would be really homesick for a few days, and then the sadness would pass. They could hear Mema's voice calling out for them to come in, so they did. After taking a shower and putting on her pj's, Karen and Bunny-Bunny sat downstairs and talked to Papa and Mema.

Mema always read some health remedy books or the Bible, or she separated her pills into daily slots (Sunday through Saturday). Mema took a lot of pills. She had a notebook with everything she took written down in it. Even when she was in the hospital, once, she told the nurse that she was missing two pills that she normally took at night. The nurse had said, "No, Mrs. Benz, I've checked off everything from your list."

Mema said, "Wait a minute, honey. I take this for that, that for this," and this back-and-forth went on for ten minutes.

Finally, the nurse said, "Mrs. Benz, you're right. I failed to give you two pills. I do apologize."

When the nurse walked out, Mema said, "Karen Willie, you must always keep up with what medicines you take because nurses and doctors are human, and they make mistakes too. But you don't have to be the patient that suffers the consequences."

Karen had never forgotten what Mema said that day, but hopefully she wouldn't have to take any medicine. This time, Mema was reading an article from today's paper. She thought it was so funny. She chuckled while she read it. Papa said, "Whatcha reading, baby?"

Mema said, "Lawrence Beamon has an interesting article in the paper today. The topic read 'Being Mean Is Not So Sweet.'"

Dear Lawrence, my uncle George never smiles. Everyone in town talks about him. People speak, and he nods his head but never says a word. Some days he looks so mean people hold their head down so they won't have to speak. Uncle George works at the bank, so everyone in town knows him. The other day, Uncle George walked down to the ice-cream shop after his lunch and had a chocolate ice-cream cone. He came back to the bank, and folks started snickering as they looked at him. He began to walk, and more people laughed. Uncle George went to the restroom, and as he walked in and looked in the mirror, he found he had chocolate ice cream on his face. Uncle George had to laugh as he licked his lips and wiped his mouth. When he came out of the restroom, he was laughing. Others were laughing too. Uncle George has been smiling ever since. Uncle George said, "Had I not been so mean, grumpy, and just simply smiled, someone might have told me I had chocolate ice cream on my face."

Mr. Lawrence said, "In this case, being mean turned out nice and chocolate sweet."

Mema said, "See, Karen, being kind and friendly is good and healthy for you and others."

Karen's mom had said that Mema was wise and had experienced a lot in life. Mema had succeeded in life because she honored and obeyed her parents. She was giving and caring. She was humble and always chose gentle words when others would yell. Mema would look at them, and they would behave. Mema's eyes could tell you how to behave, and her mouth never opened. Karen's mom had told her, "Yes, yes, Karen, your Mema is equipped with a wealth of knowledge, and if you keep an open mind, you will receive quite a bit of vital information."

Karen was tired, so she hugged Papa and Mema and went to bed.

Hard Work with Great Rewards

The aroma of maple sausage and pancakes cooking woke Karen up. She jumped up and ran downstairs.

Mema said, "Child, wash your face and brush your teeth."

Karen said, "I know, Mema. I was just so excited I forgot."

Mema had already fed Bunny-Bunny, and he was very happy. After they ate, Karen went outside to help Papa. Papa said he needed to borrow her legs today because he was tired. So he had already gotten four orders ready for the neighbors. He sold vegetables at a very low price.

Mema said, "That's what keeps Papa in good health. He's always getting enough exercise when he's working in the garden or delivering baskets of tomatoes, cucumbers, apples, pears, and watermelons."

Karen worked until noon, and then they had lunch. At lunch, Papa said because of her hard work, they would ride down to the fairgrounds where fireworks began at 7:00 p.m. Karen was so excited because North Carolina fireworks were better than back home. Mema made sure she had her earplugs, and off we went.

The fireworks started on time. They were beautiful. The first one went straight up, opened up with a white fountain in the beginning, and ended up with blue and green flickering lights. They only lasted about fifteen minutes, but they were the best ever.

On the way home, we stopped at the ice-cream parlor. I was ordering a vanilla cone when someone tapped me on my back. I turned around, and it was Sara, the neighbor's granddaughter. Sara was a lot of fun. I told her maybe we could play tomorrow after I did my chores.

Sara's Jealousy

Karen finished all her chores. She asked Mema if she could play with Sara since she finished all her chores. Mema said, "Yes, Karen, have fun. Come back around 5:00 p.m. to get cleaned up for dinner."

Karen said, "Okay."

Sara lived four homes away from Mema's house. The problem was that each house sat on at least one to two acres of land. It took Karen about ten minutes to get to Sara's house. Karen left Bunny–Bunny on the porch. As Karen walked up to Sara's door, she rang the doorbell. The door was open, but the screen door was locked. Sara came running from the backyard.

Sara said, "Karen, what do want to do today?"

Karen said, "Do you mind if we walked back to Mema's house? I don't really want to leave Bunny–Bunny."

Sara said, "Okay, let me tell Mom and get my bike."

As Karen waited, she thought about how sad Bunny–Bunny seemed when she was leaving to go to Sara's house. Bunny–Bunny was accustomed to going everywhere with Karen. It was impossible for him to go because of all the stray dogs that came after Bunny–Bunny. Karen thought to herself Bunny–Bunny would be happy to see her come back with Sara to play at Mema's house.

Sara said, "Okay, Karen, let's go." Sara had her backpack stuffed with dolls and toys.

When Karen and Sara started coming up the long winding dirt road to Mema's house, she could see Bunny-Bunny through the screened porch jumping around. Karen knew Bunny-Bunny would be happy to see her. Sara jumped off the bike and started to play tag, running around the yard tagging Karen. Bunny-Bunny was outside hopping around too. Karen said, "You're it."

Sara said, "I'm tired. Let's catch our breath."

Karen and Sara lay back on the grass. Mema's grass was like lying on the carpet. When the wind blew, you could see grass swirling back and forth. Karen began to rub Bunny-Bunny and said, "It's so much fun here at Mema's."

Sara rose from lying down and walked away.

Karen asked, "Where are you going?"

Sara said, "I'm just walking."

"What's wrong?"

"You are always talking to Bunny-Bunny and rubbing him. I know he's your pet and best friend, but I'm your friend too. At least I can talk to you. Bunny-Bunny can't talk."

"It doesn't matter if Bunny-Bunny speaks or not. I love him. I asked for a pet for so long, and when my parents finally said I could have one, I was so happy. I was so lonely before Bunny-Bunny was given to me." Bunny-Bunny was sitting back listening to everything that was said. Karen added, "Sara, why don't you ask your parents if you can have a pet?"

Sara said, "Karen, you have Bunny-Bunny every day. You only visit your grandparents for two weeks out of the year. Can you and I just have fun together?"

Karen smiled and said, "Okay." Bunny-Bunny just hopped back on the porch. Karen felt torn between Bunny-Bunny and Sara.

Day after day, Karen played more with Sara, trying to show her lots of attention. When she came home, she would try to make special time with Bunny-Bunny. One evening, Karen decided to tell Mema what Sara had said.

Karen said, "Mema, Sara gets sad when I show Bunny-Bunny a lot of attention. She told me that I have Bunny-Bunny all the time at home. She wanted me to spend more time with her since I'll be leaving soon. I asked her to see if her parents would let her get a pet. She told me no because of her mom's job and her dad's commitment to the boys' club."

Bunny-Bunny was sitting on the porch listening.

Mema said, "Listen, sweetie. Sara is jealous of Bunny-Bunny. Sara is fearful of losing her friendship with you to Bunny-Bunny. The thing is, your love for Bunny-Bunny is very special. It would take a lot for anyone to take his place. Sara is lonely because her parents have very busy schedules, and she is an only child. Jealously is a strong feeling that can sometimes consume you."

Karen said, "What do you mean consume you?"

"It can take over you if you don't learn how to handle it. So tell me, young lady, what have you done to make this situation better?"

"I've been playing with her most of the day, and what's left of the day, I play with Bunny-Bunny. Mema, I really miss Bunny-Bunny when I spend the whole day with Sara."

Mema said, "Karen, I'm sure Bunny-Bunny knows you love him. Sweetie, you have to talk to Sara and let her know you enjoy playing with her when you visit with us. Tell Sara all of you should be able to play together. I'm sure she will understand."

Two more days, and Karen's parents would be coming to take her home. Today Karen and Sara were going to play in the tree house in the backyard at Mema's house. They had all the dolls and their clothes. They must have changed the dolls' outfits at least ten times, a different outfit for each occasion. After the girls played awhile with their dolls, they started talking.

Karen said, "Sara, I just wanted to tell you that I am happy I have you to play with when I come to North Carolina. But I talked to Mema about feeling torn between playing with you and with Bunny-Bunny. I really hope that when I come back next year, we can all play together. I really love Bunny-Bunny, and I really love playing with both of you."

Sara said, "You are right, Karen. I talked to my mom about it, and she said I was jealous of Bunny-Bunny, and I said I wasn't. Mom said that when I see you with Bunny-Bunny, I felt like he was my competition. You know, I guess I felt like I wouldn't have to struggle to talk with you because sometimes you get so wrapped up in hugging and rubbing Bunny-Bunny. Mom said jealousy is not a good thing, and I needed to work on turning my jealousy around to love for Bunny-Bunny. Karen, I'm sorry I acted that way. I promise from now on I will treat Bunny-Bunny the same as you do. We will be close friends."

Karen said, "I'm so happy we talked, Sara. So can we go spend some time with Bunny-Bunny now?"

Sara said yes. Both Karen and Sara climbed down from the tree house and ran toward the house where Bunny-Bunny was jumping on the porch. It was Karen's last day with Mema. Mema promised Karen they would make cookies to take home. Mema always made a vanilla-cream pound cake for Dad. Karen and Mema baked most of the day. Sara came over just in time to have some fresh baked chocolate-chip, oatmeal-raisin, and sugar cookies. Karen and Sara enjoyed their cookies with a cold glass of milk.

After Karen and Sara ate, they played outside with Bunny-Bunny. Later that day, Karen said, "Mema, I really wish I had talked to you about Sara's jealousy earlier because playing together with Bunny-Bunny has been much more fun. I really believe Sara loves Bunny-Bunny. I don't think she is jealous anymore."

Mema said, "Karen, that's because Sara no longer feels like she is competing with Bunny-Bunny. You know, Sara doesn't feel threatened by your relationship with Bunny-Bunny. Karen, always remember you have to communicate with your parents if something becomes difficult for you to understand with your friends. As you get older, you will learn if you can't figure it out, talk it over with someone you trust who gives you good advice." Mema hugged Karen. "I'm going to miss you being around here, baby."

Karen started packing. She knew tomorrow would come fast because this was the last night at her grandparents'. Papa would always work really hard in his garden when Karen was leaving.

Mema said, "He is trying to keep busy because he doesn't want her to see how sad he is that you're leaving." Mema always had tears in her eyes when Karen was leaving, and so did she.

About the Author

Maria Williams, a native Virginian, is inspired by her ten grandchildren. Some of her experiences as a child are narrated throughout the book. She realized at a very young age that she was different from her other schoolmates. For many years, her grandchildren would read her unpublished books when they visited. Among all the books available for the grandchildren to read on the bookshelf, they always chose to read *The Adventures of Karen and Bunny-Bunny*.

CPSIA information can be obtained
at www.ICGtesting.com
Printed in the USA
LVHW070726210121
677073LV00006B/118